THE TRAGICALLY HIP

ABC

ADAPTED BY **Drew Macklin**

ILLUSTRATED BY **Clayton Hanmer, Julia Breckenreid, Bridget George and Monika Melnychuk**

tundra

A is for Ahead By A Century

B is for Bobcaygeon

C is for Courage

D is for Don't Wake Daddy

E is for Everytime You Go

F is for Fireworks

G is for Goodnight Attawapiskat

H is for At The Hundredth Meridian

I is for I'll Believe In You

J is for Just As Well

K is for The Kids Don't Get It

L is for Little Bones

M is for My Music At Work

N is for New Orleans Is Sinking

O is for Ouch

P is for Poets

Q is for Queen Of The Furrows

R is for Radio Show

S is for Silver Jet

T is for Trickle Down

U is for Use It Up

V is for In View

W is for Wheat Kings

X is for The Luxury

Y is for Yer Not The Ocean

Z is for Frozen In My Tracks

Critically acclaimed for more than three decades, **THE TRAGICALLY HIP** has been at the heart of the Canadian musical zeitgeist, evoking a strong emotional connection between their music and their fans. The five-piece group of friends includes **Rob Baker** (guitar), **Gord Downie** (vocals, guitar), **Johnny Fay** (drums), **Paul Langlois** (guitar) and **Gord Sinclair** (bass), who all grew up in Kingston, Ontario. **THE HIP** has achieved the enviable status of a band that enjoys mass popularity, with more than twelve million albums sold worldwide, while maintaining a grassroots following.

Their studio catalog includes their self-titled debut album, *The Tragically Hip* (1987); *Up to Here* (1989); *Road Apples* (1991); *Fully Completely* (1992); *Day for Night* (1994); *Trouble at the Henhouse* (1996); *Phantom Power* (1998); *Music @ Work* (2000); *In Violet Light* (2002); *In Between Evolution* (2004); *World Container* (2006); *We Are the Same* (2009); *Now for Plan A* (2012); *Man Machine Poem* (2016) and *Saskadelphia* (2021).

CLAYTON HANMER is an illustrator with a broad range of clients from the *New York Times* to *National Geographic Kids*. He has illustrated several books, including *The Museum of Odd Body Leftovers* by Rachel Poliquin. He lives in Prince Edward County, Ontario, with his family.

JULIA BRECKENREID is an illustrator who lives in Toronto, Ontario, where she paints stories for kids big and small. Her books include *An Eye for Color* by Natasha Wing and *Dorothy & Herbert* by Jackie Azúa Kramer.

BRIDGET GEORGE is an Anishinaabe author-illustrator and mom. She was raised on the shores of Lake Huron in the traditional territory of her people in Kettle and Stony Point First Nation in Ontario. *It's a Mitig!* was her debut picture book.

MONIKA MELNYCHUK has been illustrating for over twenty years, working from Toronto, Vancouver Island and Los Angeles before bringing her laptop and dog for a summer to Whitehorse, Yukon. It's been sixteen years and she never left. Her clients include Harlequin, Purolator, McDonald's, Weber Shandwick and many editorial publications and publishers.

Tundra Books, an imprint of Tundra Book Group, a division of Penguin Random House of Canada Limited

Library and Archives Canada Cataloguing in Publication available upon request.

ISBN 9781774881248 (hardcover) | ISBN 9781774881255 (EPUB)

Published simultaneously in the United States of America by Tundra Books of Northern New York,
an imprint of Tundra Book Group, a division of Penguin Random House of Canada Limited

Library of Congress Control Number: 2022947214

Edited by Samantha Swenson and Peter Phillips
Cover design by Gigi Lau
Interior design by John Martz and Gigi Lau
The text was set in Proxima Nova.

Printed in India

www.thehip.com
www.penguinrandomhouse.ca

1 2 3 4 5 27 26 25 24 23

Penguin
Random House
TUNDRA BOOKS